Bungleman

Bruntsfield Primary School
Edinburgh
EH10 4NA

Bruntsfield Primary School
5 NOV 2008
h EH10 4NA

D0543658

Written by Jeremy Strong
Illustrated by Julian Mosedale

Collins

 Bungleman, superhero

Every town needs a superhero. It doesn't have to be someone like Superman or Batman. They are more like super-duper-superheroes, and their powers are truly amazing. They are terrific at solving Big Problems – things like catching Master Criminals and preventing the End of the World.

But there are lots of smaller problems that need sorting out, too. Think about everyday problems, like finding lost pets, or helping little kids across the road. Super-duper-superheroes are far too busy to bother with them. That's when you need a more ordinary kind of superhero. Every town should have one – and Pickleton had Bungleman.

Bungleman lived at 23, Messup Road. It was a small, semi-detached house, and he lived there with his wife, Mrs Bungleman, and their son, Dennis.

Bungleman went on patrol every day. He'd get up in the morning, take a shower and pull on his superhero outfit.

Do you know why superheroes wear special clothes? There are two reasons:

1 So that you know who they are.

2 If you travel at hyper-speed, the surface of your skin starts to burn, so superheroes' outfits are there to protect them. They are flameproof.

After breakfast, Bungleman would start work. Up and up he'd zoom, whizzing across the sky like a ... well, like a superhero. The people of Pickleton would look up and see Bungleman overhead and they would feel safe and secure.

IF ONLY THEY KNEW THE TRUTH!
THEY WEREN'T SAFE AT ALL!!

They *weren't* safe because Bungleman was USELESS. He made a mess of everything. If you asked him to cut the grass, he'd probably mow the flowerbeds. If you asked him to put the ironing away, he'd shut himself in the wardrobe.

Why didn't people notice that he was useless? Well, they didn't notice because every time Bungleman made a mess of things, someone came to his rescue. Guess who it was?

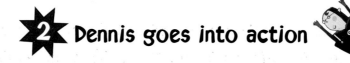

It was Dennis.

There was that business with Miss Toggle, for example. It was something Miss Toggle would rather forget. If it hadn't been for Dennis, she would have been the most embarrassed head teacher in Pickleton. Miss Toggle was having a lovely, frothy bubble bath when she managed to get her big toe stuck up the hot tap. Luckily, she had her mobile with her and she dialled up Bungleman's number: 3-2-1-GO. That instantly set an alarm flashing on Bungleman's master map of Pickleton.

"Miss Toggle's in deadly danger!" cried Bungleman, putting on his superhero outfit inside out. "Clear the room, it's time to zoom!"

A moment later – **whooooosh!** He was off!

If only he'd opened the window before he whizzed through it.

"You'd better follow your dad," said Mrs Bungleman.
"You know what he's like."

Dennis scrambled into his own, rather baggy superhero
pants and whizzed off after his dad.

Bungleman had gone straight off to Miss Toggle. He came
crashing down through the bathroom ceiling. He could see
what was wrong at once. What he needed to do was to take
the tap off. How could he do that? He needed a tool from
the DIY shop. So what did Bungleman do? He picked up
the bath, still full of bubbles and Miss Toggle, carried it
across to the DIY shop and plonked it down outside, where
everyone could see.

"Oooh!" went poor Miss Toggle. She slid down as far as
she could go beneath the bubbles without drowning.

Luckily, Dennis wasn't far behind. While Bungleman was in the shop, Dennis shot down, grabbed the bath, and put it on the roof of the DIY shop where nobody could see. Miss Toggle was very grateful but rather surprised at how small Bungleman had suddenly become.

"You've shrunk," she said.

"Every time I use my superpowers I get a little smaller," Dennis explained quickly. Then he blushed, because he'd just broken the Superhero Code of Conduct, Rule Number One: a superhero never lies.

He flew off to make sure that his dad found the bath all right and could sort out Miss Toggle's stuck toe.

Then there was the time Bungleman had to round up an elephant that had escaped from the zoo. He chased it inside the Pickleton Hotel, where it got into a lift and promptly whizzed up to the top floor. Bungleman frantically poked the call button to get the lift back down.

Meanwhile, Dennis saw what to do. He raced upstairs and found the elephant just stepping out of the lift.
He hypnotised the elephant by staring at it with his eyes crossed.

"You will obey my every command," droned Dennis (in fluent elephant language, of course), staring into the elephant's eyes.

"I will obey," echoed the elephant (also in elephant language).

10

"Go downstairs and obey my father," Dennis growled. The elephant turned and padded downstairs. Bungleman was surprised, but very pleased to see the elephant.

"Aha! Just as I thought. I sent out a silent command and the elephant has obeyed. He is in my power," smiled Dennis's dad.

"Hooray!" shouted the crowd. "Hooray for Bungleman!"

Meanwhile Dennis went quietly home, shaking his head. Honestly! His dad was hopeless!

3 Dennis is fed up

Dennis was fed up. What was the point of being useful and clever? He knew he couldn't tell anyone about it. If the town found out that his dad was useless, they would laugh at the whole family forever. He would never live it down. Dennis had to keep quiet so no one would guess.

Most of the time he didn't care, but he did wish that he could use some of his superpowers at school.

He could do amazing things for his dad, but he couldn't even use a supercalculator to get his sums right. (Superhero Code of Conduct, Rule Number Two: superheroes must not use superpowers except when doing superhero work.)

Dennis wasn't very good at maths and he wasn't all that good at writing. He tended to make lots of mistakes. And, if you tend to make mistakes at football, people notice. Once he'd scored a goal. A shame he'd scored in his own net! Poor Dennis.

Dennis was nine. He looked a bit like his father, except that he was younger, smaller and much cleverer.

Dennis's mother had made his superhero outfit out of one of Bungleman's own suits. She had cut down the cape to size, but sadly, she couldn't make the pants any smaller because, as you probably know, superheroes' superpowers are kept in their pants. So the pants had to stay the same size, which made them far too big. Dennis had to use a belt and braces to hold them up.

He felt totally stupid, but he put up with it because nobody must ever know about his dad being useless – not even his dad. After all, Bungleman was very proud of his job.

Do you see how awful it was for Dennis? One moment he'd be racing through the sky, saving Pickleton from disaster (and his dad), and the next, he'd be back at school, being moaned at. Worst of all, he couldn't tell anyone about his bravery. No one knew that Dennis had to put things right when his dad got them wrong!

4 The Great Kitchen Emergency

Then came the day of the Great Kitchen Emergency.
It started just like any other day. The children were in their classrooms, Miss Toggle was snoring in her office, and the cooks were in the kitchen, making lunch. They were using giant bowls and giant machines of every kind. Outside, the sky grew darker and darker. A storm was brewing.

All at once: **KERRANNNNGGGG!**

An enormous flash of lightning split the sky and hit the school kitchen. One cook's hair stood on end and turned white, instantly. Cook number two was blown right across the kitchen and landed in a giant bowl of custard. And cook number three's apron flipped right up over her head. "I can't see! I can't see!" she moaned, walking straight into a cupboard and knocking over six shelves of saucepans.

As if that wasn't bad enough, all the electric machines in the kitchen got supercharged with electricity and took on a life of their own. The giant mixer began to spin across the floor, dragging things into its beaters and ripping them to shreds. The potato chipping machine was pumping out chips like bullets, spraying them at cook number four. The juicer was mashing fruit and veg and squirting out tomato-coloured goo like a liquid flame-thrower.

The cooks dashed out of the kitchen, slipping and sliding on the food-spattered floor, chased by the monster machines. Their screams and yells brought the teachers running to the rescue. The machines turned instantly upon their new victims.

Three hundred high-speed chips mowed down Miss Toggle. Mr Brownlow and Mrs Woodbegood were blown off their feet by a jet of tomato sludge.

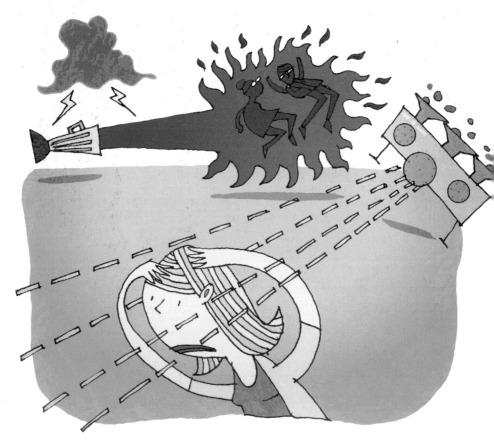

The teachers had to retreat. Miss Toggle hid behind a wheelie bin and hurriedly dialled 3-2-1-GO!

"We need you, Bungleman!" she cried desperately, as a fountain of sludge landed on top of her head.

Back at number 23, Bungleman leaped from his chair. "Clear the room, it's time to zoom!" he cried.

"I'll open the window for you," Mrs Bungleman said. She watched anxiously as her husband whizzed off. "I do hope Dennis is there to help," she said to herself.

Of course Dennis was there. He knew at once that something terrible was happening on the far side of the school and that meant Dad would need his help. He had to get out of the classroom and change into his baggy pants. Dennis had often had to do this.

He put up his hand and used his usual excuse. "Can I go to the toilet, please?" he asked his teacher.

"Dennis Bungleman, I have never known a child go to the toilet as often as you do," his teacher complained. "Must you really go?"

"Yes," said Dennis. "Or something awful will happen."

The teacher definitely did not want something awful to happen. "All right," she sighed. "Off you go, again."

Dennis went to the toilets, climbed into his baggy pants and set off. Sometimes, he felt like a babysitter.

It was a good thing that Dennis was there, because things were already going wrong for Bungleman.

Bungleman was very good at catching chips and throwing them back. But then the chips got caught up in the mixer, were instantly shredded and spat out again – and now that they'd been shredded, there were ten times more of them. Meanwhile, Bungleman had been hit by a splat of sludge and got a bit of minced carrot in his eye. He couldn't see properly. Blinking rapidly, he went to find Miss Toggle.

"I've got something in my eye," he moaned.
"Can you help?"

This was not the sort of behaviour Miss Toggle had come to expect from a superhero and besides, she was covered from head to toe in sludge and chips.

Bungleman staggered off to the toilets. Standing in front of a mirror, he tried to get the carrot out using the corner of his cape like a hanky.

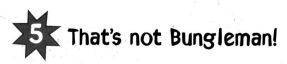

5 That's not Bungleman!

Dennis saw his chance. He came hurtling out of the sky like a flash of lightning (wearing baggy pants). He grabbed a dinner tray and jammed it into the mixer. The beaters instantly got stuck and the engine exploded.

He chucked a couple of bricks into the chipper. It coughed twice, choked, died and toppled onto its side. As for the juicer, Dennis simply whacked the switch and it stopped. So that was that.

HISSSSSSSS!

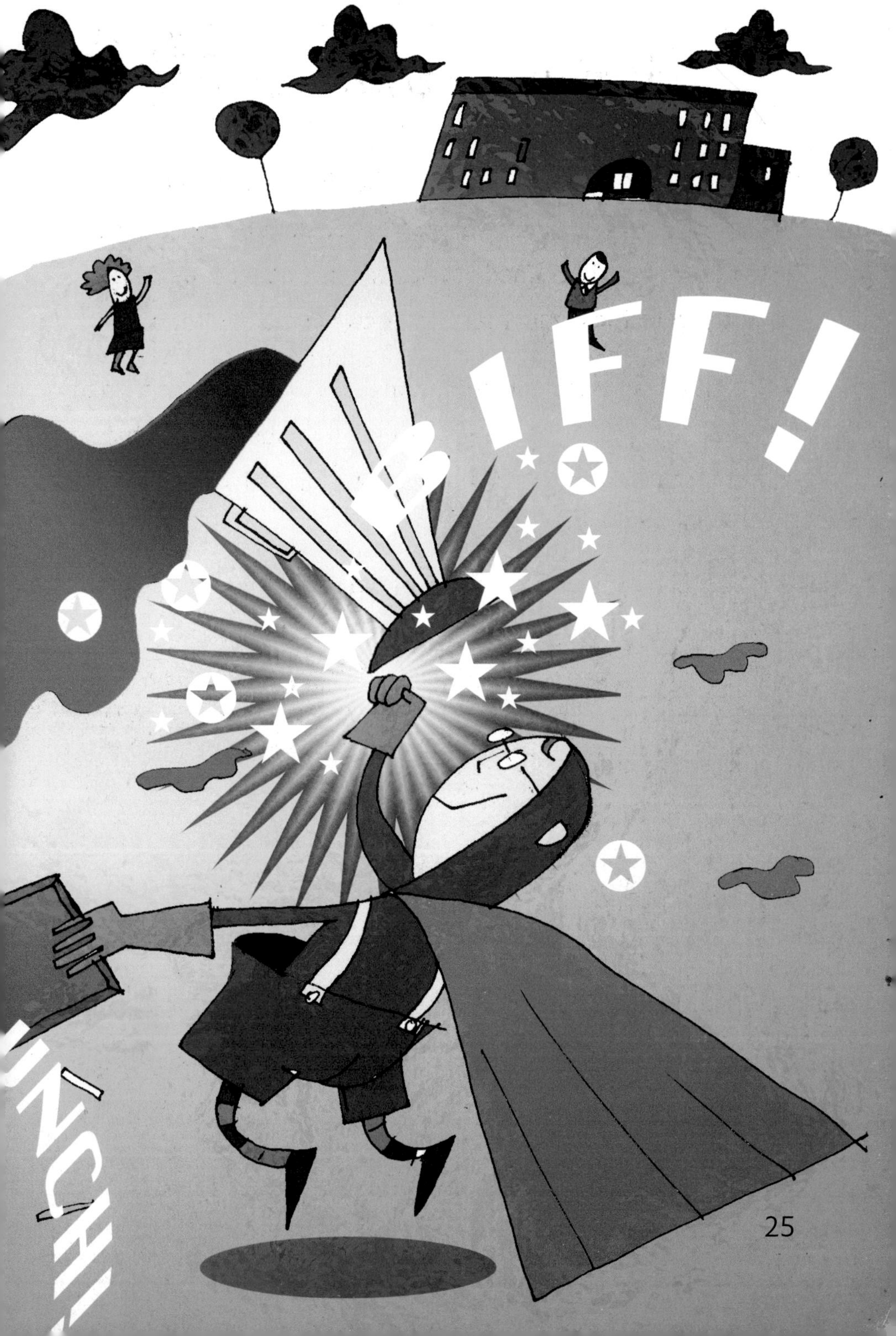
BIFF!

The teachers and children crept out from their hiding places. For a few seconds they just stared at the mess around them. Then they began cheering, "Hooray! Hooray for Bungleman!"

"That's not Bungleman," said one little girl. "Bungleman is much bigger."

"That IS Bungleman," said Miss Toggle. "When he uses his superpowers, he gets smaller and smaller. He told me so himself."

At that moment, the real Bungleman came out of the toilets. He'd finally got the carrot out of his eye and he was ready to do battle again. Everyone stared at him. Then they stared at Dennis.

"THAT'S Bungleman," said the little girl.
"And that's Dennis."

"Dennis?" shouted everyone else. "But he's useless!"
And that was when Bungleman – the real Bungleman –
became a proper superhero.

Bungleman stepped forward. "Dennis is NOT useless,"
he said. "You don't think I can tackle major emergencies
like this on my own, do you? Everyone needs a helper, and
I have my son, Dennis. Without his help, I couldn't be
Bungleman at all."

The crowd gazed at Dennis. He did *look* useless. But that
was only because he was wearing his dad's baggy pants.
Who had blipped the chipper? Who had beaten the beaters?
Who had whacked the juicer? Dennis.

The little girl suddenly ran forward and threw her arms round Dennis's knees. (She was quite small.)

"I love Dennis!" she cried. "I'm going to marry him!"

"Steady on," murmured Bungleman. "He's only nine."

But the crowd didn't care. Dennis had saved them – Dennis, Son of Bungleman. They cheered and cheered and all of a sudden, Dennis knew he wasn't useless any more.

He wasn't Dennis any more either, because from that day on, everyone called him Bungleboy.

A Venn diagram

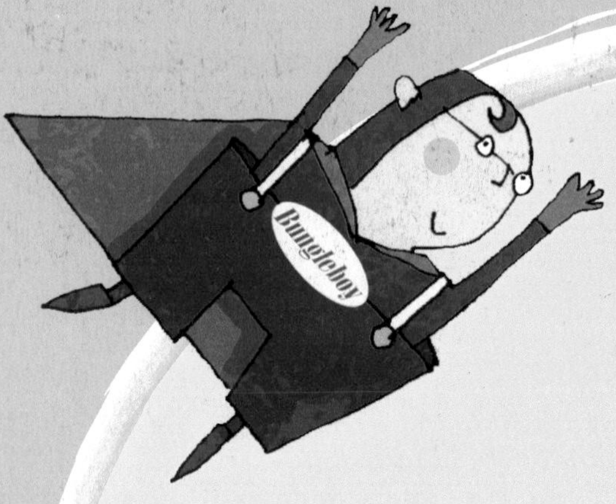
Bungleboy

clears up after his dad

doesn't get credit for his actions

is a small superhero

often feels useless

are both superheroes

want to help others

Dennis

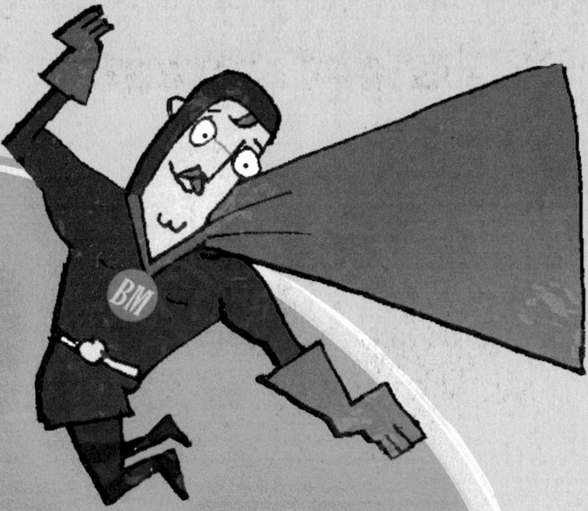
BM

are both brave

want to protect their family

causes chaos when trying to save the day

gets credit for his actions

is a full-size superhero

feels heroic

Bungleman

⁂ Ideas for guided reading ⁂

Learning objectives: how dialogue is presented in stories; be aware of the different voices in stories using dramatised readings, showing differences between the narrator and different characters used; the basic conventions of speech; present events and characters through dialogue to engage the interest of an audience

who help us - the local police; ICT: Writing stories: communicating information using text

Interest words: hyper-speed, flameproof, DIY, conduct, hypnotised, droned, fluent, obey, echoed, supercalculator, supercharged, desperately, anxiously, emergencies

Curriculum links: Art and design: People in action; Citizenship: People

Resources: whiteboards or scrap paper and pencils/pens

Getting started

This book can be read over two or more guided reading sessions.

- Ask them to name any superheroes they know. *What are his/her special powers? Can a superhero's name gives clues about these special powers, e.g. Spiderman?*

- Introduce the title and ask the group to guess this superhero's special powers.

- Ask them to read chapter 1 silently to get some background information about Bungleman.

- Draw attention to the top of p7 and discuss the use of speech marks. Experiment with voices for Bungleman and model how to read speech, differentiating clearly between speech and narration.

Reading and responding

- Ask the children to return to the beginning of chapter 2 and begin to read silently at their own pace. Ask them to read pieces of speech out loud as they come to them. Check that they are attempting to use different voices for new characters.